Dear Parent:

Congratulations! Your child is taking the first steps on an exciting journey. The destination? Independent reading!

STEP INTO READING® will help your child get there. The program offers five steps to reading success. Each step includes fun stories and colorful art. There are also Step into Reading Sticker Books, Step into Reading Math Readers, Step into Reading Phonics Readers, Step into Reading Write-In Readers, and Step into Reading Phonics Boxed Sets—a complete literacy program with something to interest every child.

Learning to Read, Step by Step!

Ready to Read   Preschool–Kindergarten
• big type and easy words • rhyme and rhythm • picture clues
For children who know the alphabet and are eager to begin reading.

Reading with Help   Preschool–Grade 1
• basic vocabulary • short sentences • simple stories
For children who recognize familiar words and sound out new words with help.

Reading on Your Own   Grades 1–3
• engaging characters • easy-to-follow plots • popular topics
For children who are ready to read on their own.

Reading Paragraphs   Grades 2–3
• challenging vocabulary • short paragraphs • exciting stories
For newly independent readers who read simple sentences with confidence.

Ready for Chapters   Grades 2–4
• chapters • longer paragraphs • full-color art
For children who want to take the plunge into chapter books but still like colorful pictures.

STEP INTO READING® is designed to give every child a successful reading experience. The grade levels are only guides. Children can progress through the steps at their own speed, developing confidence in their reading, no matter what their grade.

Remember, a lifetime love of reading starts with a single step!

Copyright © 2011 Disney/Pixar. All rights reserved. Slinky® Dog is a registered trademark of Poof-Slinky, Inc. © Poof-Slinky, Inc. Mr. Potato Head® and Mrs. Potato Head® are registered trademarks of Hasbro, Inc. Used with permission. © Hasbro, Inc. All rights reserved. Mattel toys used with permission. © Mattel Inc. All rights reserved. Published in the United States by Random House Children's Books, a division of Random House, Inc., 1745 Broadway, New York, NY 10019, and in Canada by Random House of Canada Limited, Toronto, in conjunction with Disney Enterprises, Inc.

Step into Reading, Random House, and the Random House colophon are registered trademarks of Random House, Inc.

Visit us on the Web!
StepIntoReading.com
www.randomhouse.com/kids
Educators and librarians, for a variety of teaching tools, visit us at
www.randomhouse.com/teachers

ISBN 978-0-7364-2738-8 (trade)
ISBN 978-0-7364-8088-8 (lib. bdg.)

Printed in the United States of America   10 9 8 7 6 5 4 3 2

Random House Children's Books supports the First Amendment and celebrates the right to read.

DISNEY · PIXAR

TOY STORY

MOVE OUT!

Adapted by Apple Jordan

Based on an original story by Jason Katz

Illustrated by Allan Batson and
the Disney Storybook Artists

Random House 🏠 New York

Andy is grown up.
He does not play
with his toys anymore.

The Green Army Men
have a plan.
Sarge tells his troops
to move out!
They salute Woody
and Buzz.

Then the troops jump
out the window.
They soar into the air.

They will find

a new home.

The troops land
at a toy store.
Sarge looks for a child
to take them home.

Inside the store,
Sarge sees a boy.

The troops hide
in the boy's bag.
They will go home
with him!

But the boy
does not go home.
He goes
to a bakery.

The boy drops his bag.
The troops fall
on the floor.
They look around.

A baker sees the troops.
He puts them
on a birthday cake.

He puts the cake
in the freezer.
The troops are cold!

The next day,
the cake goes
to a birthday party.

Sarge sees a boy.
Sarge has a plan!
The troops will
go home
with the boy.

Sarge watches the boy.

The troops wait.

The boy leaves

Pizza Planet.

The troops run
after the boy.
But he is too fast.
They cannot catch up.

Sarge spots
a pizza truck.
The truck can catch up
to the boy!

Sarge gives an order.
The troops jump
on board.

The truck speeds away
with the troops.
But it is windy
on the truck.

The troops
are blown
into the air!

The troops land
at a gas station.

They set up camp

for the night.

The next morning,
Sarge hears a loud noise.
He is lifted
into a garbage can!

Then Sarge is tossed
into a garbage truck.
The truck drives away.

Sarge's troops
will rescue him!
They make a chain.
They reach for Sarge.
Sarge is safe!

Sarge and the troops
jump off the truck.
They land
by a playground.

The troops meet
a group of toys.
They are
at Sunnyside Daycare.

There are kids
at Sunnyside.
At last, the troops
have a new home!